OMELAS REVISITED

A DYSTOPIAN FANTASY NOVELLA

C. S. Johnson

Ebook ISBN: 978-1-948464-67-3
Hardback ISBN: 978-1-948464-68-0

DEDICATION:

This is for my supporters and (Almost) Famous Readers. I am truly grateful for you, and even in a fallen world, you are a spark of perfection's light and love for me.

All the best,
CJ

OMELAS REVISITED

A DYSTOPIAN FANTASY NOVELLA

C. S. Johnson

± ± ± ±

THE ONES WHO SEE

PART ONE

± ± ± ±

The only dark moments of my life always came just after waking up.

Ever since I was twelve, there were mornings I would lie on my bed, my body stiff and unmoving, as I opened my eyes. An invisible tension shifted all around me—holding me, trapping me, possibly smothering me. The first time I'd felt it, I had refrained from saying anything, believing it to be my imagination; the City Elders had warned us about that, after all, and there was no reason to think there was cause for concern.

But the strange moments persisted.

Three years later, I still had moments in the shady mornings when I felt an unnamable otherness settle around me. Still I did not see it, I could only sense it; I did not touch it, but I could not escape the feeling I was being watched—perhaps even watched over. I could only see the shadows, and it seemed I could only see the shadows of things that were not there.

The last day of my childhood was no exception.

That morning, I stared at the ceiling and again saw nothing, but I knew there was not nothing there, either. The walls of my already small room seemed to constrict as I glanced around.

My room was cool but cozy, with whitewashed walls and clean floors, built into a small, perfect square. Off to the side was my one dresser that housed my pristine, freshly-pressed clothes, including my newest dress for the Learning Ceremony, and tucked away beside it was my one pair of constantly-shined boots. There was nothing and no one else in my room that should have made me feel afraid.

Surrounded by the gifts from my community—the boots, the clothes, the other small things I freely used, like my toothbrush and my hairbrush and even the small sewing kit my House Mother gave to me last year—I should have felt only safe and happy.

After all, these were the familiar staples of the City and its residents. Every child I knew had the exact same sort of room as I did. We valued conformity as much as community, and our large housing structures were comfortable daily reminders that we were all special, we were all needed, and all of us had a place.

All of us in the City by the Sea reveled in the security of that beauty. Our lives were happy, safe, meaningful, and peaceful. We had everything we needed and everything we could want.

So I was not sure why the last shades of early morning made everything familiar seem suddenly foreign enough to cause me to clench my one blanket to my chest and do my best to ignore it.

Occasionally, I would stare back at the shadow, trying to be brave. A few times, I would reach up and trace the outline of the shard in my forehead. It was hard and solid, smooth and comforting. The shard marked me as a member of the Community as much as it reminded me of who I was individually—where I came from, and where I was needed. At that reminder, my fear would suddenly whisk itself away.

I did not want to tell anyone about those moments; I did not want others to think I was frightened or troubled.

"Skyla, are you awake?"

My House Mother stood outside my room. The door muffled her voice, but I would have recognized it anywhere. It was the same loving, gentle tone I had known all my life.

"Yes, Mother Annika." My heart swelled with joy as I heard the same echoes of my mother's dulcet pitch in my own voice.

"You may need a few extra moments to get ready today. If you are awake, you should start moving."

Even though she could not see me, I beamed with delight.

Today marked the end of my schooling years and signaled the beginning of my new life as a contributing member of my community—the day I had anticipated for as long as I could remember.

The smile stayed firmly on my face as I hurried to the domicile's only bathroom.

And then it happened.

In a flash, like a slice of a dream, I fell forward, tripping over my flighty, impatient feet. My face collided with the hard floor, my nose smashing into the clean, spotless tile with a sharp, distinctive *crack*. I tasted warm, fresh blood; I felt the pain of broken bones, loosened teeth, and unexpected shame.

But then I blinked, and I was standing up again, right where I had stood before I had felt myself fall.

I was no longer smiling.

I touched my nose, running my hands over the rounded bump in its middle, to the short, pointed end. There was no blood. There was no pain.

There was only a shadow.

I blinked again, and found myself in the bathroom, gazing into the mirror.

Nothing is wrong.

It was silly to think there would be.

After all, I lived in the City by the Sea; some say it used to be called Omelas, but I could not remember if that was the case, or if someone came from another city called

Omelas and started this one. My peers in school agreed that "City by the Sea" was much more poetic, and it had less connection to the Imperfect Past of humanity's previous age; no one liked thinking of that topic. We learned of it in school only in our final year, along with the other names of imperfections that no longer existed. But everyone was much happier when we were able to move on, and no one had any other questions about it.

The past was the past; it did not have any bearing on the present, and we were all content to believe that.

The moment passed, and I turned my attention back to the mirror. The shard in the middle of my forehead winked at me as I watched it. The shard was more like a jewel, shaped like a small pentagon, no more than an inch in each direction. I'd always thought mine was a good fit for me, like a diamond resting on my brow.

I giggled as I pressed down on it, enjoying how the color swirled, twisting into different shades of blue and green, and even a spark of purple as the last of my worries faded.

This is who I am.

Calm and satisfied, I looked over the rest of my reflection. My face was full of unimposing beauty. My eyes were light-colored; my hair was much darker. While several of my peers had curls, I did not have as much as they did; my skin was also darker than some, but still lighter than others. My nose was straight, with the almost imperceptibly small bump on its bridge. I ran my fingers over it again, wondering about the fall and how I had felt the bridge of my nose break.

I frowned. What had happened, exactly? Or rather, what had *never* happened, exactly?

Why didn't my nose actually break? Was it the shadows, or was it just my imagination?

Strange.

Maybe I would find out later, I thought, suddenly excited. The Learning Ceremony was central to the Summer Festival. It happened every year, just after sundown, and all those who were too young were sent home and put to bed. Those who completed their education participated in the Learning Ceremony and emerged from it as full Community Members.

At that, I forgot all about my nose, and my face, and everything else. I changed into my new dress, donned my shoes, and headed down to the dining hall where First Meal was being served.

"Skyla, you look lovely." My House Mother, Annika, gave me a glowing smile as she handed me a plate of bread.

I flushed with pleasure. Mother Annika was very lovely, both gentle in her appearance and humble in her manners. She was one of the younger House Mothers, still in her thirties, and I enjoyed being part of her house. Before I could give her my thanks, both for the compliment and the food, another voice spoke up.

"She should, after all the extra time she had in the bathroom."

My smile only widened as I looked at River. With a similar facial structure and only slightly darker hair, my brother was close to a year older than me ("one year, two weeks, and six days," as he would remind me from time to time), but since he had arrived into the Mercer House just after the Summer Festival, we were the same age. Even though he was technically born earlier, he never seemed to mind being in the same class as me—or so I thought.

A slim half-second passed in which he scowled at me, his eyes narrow and his tongue sticking out in clear displeasure.

But then the second passed, and his face instantly righted itself into his usual, jovial expression. His own cerulean-colored shard, embedded in his forehead just the same as mine, gleamed with only happiness.

I frowned, curious at the flicker of another imagining, but River did not seem to notice my concern.

"Are you excited for tonight, Sky? The Ceremony's going to be great," River said. "Aidan told me that it's life-changing."

"Oh, Aidan said that?" I sat down beside River, who chatted easily about Aiden, his closest friend and a member of the Aeros House, our neighbor to the right.

With his bright, sun-colored hair and his ice-like eyes, Aiden was a month older than River, but he had arrived before the Summer Festival, so he was considered seventeen by the Community. That made him nearly two years older than me. I appreciated Aidan and the companionship he provided my brother and me. We had grown up near each other, playing in the same hidden caves by the shoreline, going to the same school, and participating in the Community's numerous events.

Now that we were older, Aidan had an official job with the Community, and it was my part-time duty to help Aidan's House Mother, Erika, and her young child, Storm. When I went to their domicile, he would always give me a gracious nod.

There were other things about him I liked, too, even if they were not real.

Once I thought I saw him wink at me, after telling me I looked nice. Another time when I was washing Storm's baby bottles in the sink, I felt a hand ruffle my hair affectionately. I'd thought I'd seen Aidan come up beside me out of the corner of my eye, but when I turned to face him, no one was there.

But even if those things didn't really happen, I liked to think they did. As a full member of the Community, Aidan would be allowed to start his own House one day, and it was possible he would choose me for a House Mother when he was old enough to be allowed to add children.

There was a knock at the front door, and, as if I'd conjured him up by the mere thought, Aidan appeared at our door. I hurriedly gulped down the rest of my water, stuffing the last bit of bread into my mouth. A rush of pleasure ran through me as I remembered I was wearing my new dress, the white one trimmed with lace. Once the Learning Ceremony was over, I would receive a circlet of flowers and lace I could wear in my hair.

"I was just thinking of heading your way," River said, giving Aidan's hand a friendly squeeze in welcome.

"Mother Aeros came to ask me to see if Skyla would be able to come early today," Aidan said.

I whirled around to face him, almost coughing as I swallowed a large lump of half-chewed crust. I hurried to compose myself, unsure of why I suddenly felt nervous.

The twists in my belly and the burning by my ears evaporated in the next moment, as Aidan and River continued to talk.

"I have also been sent to ask if River would come and assist with the Learning

Ceremony setup," Aidan said. "Lady Sula said it is good for us to help out today."

"The Lead Elder asked us to help?" River's eyes widened with excitement.

"We are well aware of how important the Ceremony is to our incoming members," Aiden replied.

"That is true. I imagine it is also very helpful for the new members, knowing as they do about the Ceremony," Mother Annika agreed. "What a good way to channel your efforts to help those who are so innocently eager."

I almost frowned at her remark. What did she mean by that?

Before I could ask—or even think of asking—Mother Annika waved her arm, gesturing toward our house's daily ration of bread and a container of purified water. "Can I offer you anything to eat or drink before you go?"

"No, thank you." Aidan looked back at me, as I quickly wiped off my dishes into the sink. "Once Skyla is ready, we should head out. Mother Erika is eager to help set up for the Feast that will take place after the Learning Ceremony."

"Your House Mother is the Community's best baker, Aidan," River said.

There was a silent second where we all seemed to be holding our breath, and then Aidan spoke.

"She is just as gifted as your own," Aidan replied, swiftly covering for my brother's crudely worded statement.

"Thank you," Mother Annika said. I saw the shard in her forehead glimmer, this time colored with a strange mix of contentment and contrition; a second passed, and then she smiled brightly, but somehow blandly, too.

River began talking about what he'd heard about the Ceremony, and I finished setting up the dish sanitizer.

"I'm ready," I spoke up, diverting their attention back to me. River sighed as he was interrupted, but Aidan was as calm and welcoming as he had always been. On some level—the same deep, hidden level inside of me, the one where I kept the secret of my morning shadows and how I could see things that never truly happened—I wondered why Aidan got along so well with my brother. River was energetic and always enthusiastic; he always had something to say. As long as I'd known Aidan, he'd been quiet and thoughtful. His words seemed well-chosen, picked as carefully as a House Father might prepare a friendship bouquet for his chosen House Mother.

They were both good, but still so different. I had to wonder if they were truly compatible, even though I knew everyone in the Community tolerated and supported each other.

I put down my towel just as River started peppering Aidan with questions regarding the Ceremony. They left our residence while I said my farewells to my House Mother.

"Goodbye, Mother Annika," I said, leaning over to give her a quick kiss on the cheek as she packed up our remaining ration.

Mother Annika paused, letting her fingers slide over the skin where I'd kissed her. She cleared her throat a moment later, and then, with tears in her eyes, she nodded.

"Goodbye, Skyla," she whispered. "You've always been such a good girl."

"Thank you."

She tucked a stray half-curl of my hair behind my ear. "I will see you after the Learning Ceremony is over."

"Yes, Mother." I waved once more and then skipped out the door to our domicile, hurrying to catch up to River and Aidan.

"Come on, Aidan, can't you just tell me what the big surprise the Elders have for us in the Learning Ceremony is?" River's voice was a high-pitched whine, and a hearty giggle escaped me as I came up behind them.

"Calm down, River," I said. "I'm the one who has to watch over the baby today, not Aidan."

Before I could say anything, that feeling overcame me again, and life that should not have happened came to pass.

In the blink of an eye, River glared at me, looking as furious as any of the pictures of the Imperfect Past leaders. He kicked out his foot, splattering my new dress with a slosh of mud. I felt the tears form behind my eyes, before they were shuffled away by an unseen hand.

I stared ahead, forcing myself to watch, as River's body paused, his foot still in mid-air from his supposed kick; the next half-second he righted himself, and the mud was lifted off my skirt as if nature was reversing its actions.

A moment later, River beamed at me, all friendliness and smiles once more.

"You're so funny, Sky," he bantered back. "You know you'll always be the baby between us!" He reached out to affectionately pat my head, and then he continued walking, as if nothing happened.

Which, I reminded myself, as I looked down at my dress, was true.

Nothing happened.

Nothing happened, and that was what I was content to believe.

Until I saw Aidan.

There was a look on his face that made my heart begin to race as my feet stayed still.

"You saw it, didn't you?" he asked. His voice was slightly cracked with incredulity, but the consistent lull of his words remained.

I nodded, and I saw the jewel in his forehead—a fiery amber, almost like a flame frozen in rock—burn with forbidden anger.

And then before I could say or do anything else, Aidan grabbed a hold of River by the upper arm, dragging him back to face us.

"What is it?" River asked.

Aidan's fingers balled into a fist. He launched his punch into River's jaw, and at the sight of blood in my brother's mouth, I felt the scream rise inside of me.

My cry was killed almost instantly, disappearing as quickly as it had come. A second later, Aidan was only standing there, giving River a high-five while they laughed.

"What's this about?" River asked. "Did Sky forget how to congratulate someone?"

I looked from River—no longer bleeding, no apparent evidence of what had not happened—to Aidan, who looked at me intensely, more provocatively and more intently than I had ever been looked at before.

"I know your House Mother is waiting." I heard myself speak the words, even if I did not feel them come out of my mouth. "I will see you at the Ceremony later. Goodbye, and have a good time setting up everything!"

My eyes were still wide as I hurried away. My feet seemed to carry me with a will of their own. I did not want to believe what I'd thought I'd seen. I did not want to think that

Aidan was the kind of person who would hit my brother, or that my brother was the kind of person who might have deserved to be hit. I'd never seen such intentional harm caused by a human, and I was aghast at the terror I felt.

It was worse, too, because I'd had such high respect for Aidan.

"Skyla, there you are." Erika, Aidan's House Mother next door, waved to me as I approached. She gave me a smile, and the trauma I'd felt over Aidan's actions dispersed at once. "Storm has been waiting for you! She's excited to see you."

"I'm sure she would rather have you," I replied, trying to force myself back into the normal routine. There was a pounding between my eyes, just behind the shard in my forehead.

"Oh, of course not!" Erika's eyes filled with mirth as she handed me her baby girl. "She knows her House Mother needs to go and help with the Festival."

I forgot about anything terrible as I held baby Storm. She was nearly six months old, still a baby, but growing so well. She already had curlier hair than I did, but her eyes were close in color to mine. I wondered if they made Aidan think of me.

And then I felt terrible again.

"You'll be a full Community Member after today," Erika said. "Do you think you will want to be a House Mother, too, Skyla? You do very well with Storm."

"I will wait to be assigned and approved by the Community," I said. It was an automatic answer, one I was eager to fulfill. I did not yet know what my place would be in the Community, but I knew it was something they would need, and that was enough for me to be eager to embrace it.

"The Community Elders will know what is best for you," Erika said.

"Yes, I am sure they will," I agreed.

"This means you will choose to stay in the City by the Sea after the Learning Ceremony, then."

"Where else would I go?" I asked the question facetiously, with a playful grin, having no other answer for myself. I had forgotten about that part of the Learning Ceremony.

Each Community Member was someone who had chosen to stay in the City by the Sea. There were some who choose to walk away from the City after the Ceremony, but I did not have any inkling as to why they would.

The City life was perfect, and all of my family was here—River, Mother Mercer, my House Father, Albert, Aidan, and all of my peers at school. I did not know of life without them or without this place.

All of who I am is here, and this is where I belong.

Where could I go?

Where else *would* I go?

"You're so adorable," Erika cooed as she patted the baby on her head. "You're such a good girl, my little Storm. I will see you later!"

Storm merely gurgled back as her House Mother left. She did not make any fuss. The small shard on her head changed in a whirlwind of color, shining different shades of red, blue, and yellow as I tended to her.

Storm was a gift, to me as well as the Community, and over the next several hours, I could forget all the things that might have weighed me down. She would giggle and gurgle and coo and cuddle, and I was lost the moment I looked into her young and innocent eyes.

I had just finished up her afternoon feeding when the door to the Aeros house opened, and Aidan walked in. Immediately, I recalled my earlier troubles.

"Aidan."

My body went stiff, as if I was trying to figure out if I was going to be brave or if I was merely going to wait for my uncertainty to pass.

"Skyla, can you come with me?" He held out his hand to me, and I bristled.

"No," I snapped, before I could think through anything else. "Not after what you did earlier."

Aidan seemed shocked at my tone, and even I was a little surprised at how forceful I sounded. He frowned, but there was a hopeful look in his eyes that made me pause.

"I am surprised you remember what happened," he finally said.

"How could I forget?" I put my hands on my hips. "You hit my brother!"

"I *didn't*," he said, but when I shook my head, he sighed. "Okay, I did, but he didn't feel it, and he doesn't remember it, does he?"

"That doesn't make it good," I huffed, although I was not sure if that was true.

"I'm surprised you remember this morning at all," he said softly. "You never remember anything that happens between us."

My cheeks began to burn, and I suddenly began to wonder if those earlier moments—those dreams, those imaginings—were more. And, from the expression on his face, I had a feeling there were indeed a lot more.

"What is going on?" My voice was a desperate whisper as I dared to voice my uncertainty.

"You've grown up," Aidan whispered back, taking another step toward me.

"But I haven't been to the Ceremony yet," I said. "I mean, I know it's today, but—"

"Who decides what it means to grow up?" Aidan asked. "There are other things that happen in our lives that let us make those choices besides… besides things like the Community."

I saw the shard on his forehead begin to flicker, reminding me of how I had fallen and broken my nose, but I did not really fall—I thought of those things again.

Have Aidan and I talked about this before?

Storm screeched loudly, more loudly than I'd ever heard her, and began to wriggle uncontrollably. I had to set her down in her baby chair. Instantly, she calmed down and went back to her bubbly self.

My mind was only focused on getting her to be as happy as she could be for the next moment. It was so unusual for her to be upset at all. As I comforted her, everything else fell to the side; I forgot everything we discussed, and I was unable to be distracted.

Only when Storm was finally back to her happy self did I look back at Aidan. He was gazing out of the window, staring at the sunlight. He seemed to be mulling over a decision. A second before I could ask him what he was thinking, he snapped his attention back to me.

"Can you come with me?" Aidan asked. He held out his hand out to me, his palm facing up.

My mind was blank. "What we were talking about?"

"You were going to come with me," he said.

"No I wasn't," I said, suddenly indignant. I remembered how he hit River again, although I could not exactly remember why. "You hit my brother."

"I'll hit him again if you don't come with me."

"Excuse me?" The direct starkness of his words, and their uniqueness among my memory, conveyed enough gravity that I balked.

"Please, Sky," he whispered again. His eyes were suddenly soft and gentle, and his voice was full of urgent pleading. "I need you to keep fighting. Please, come with me."

I did not know what he meant, but I was determined to find out. I slowly gave him my hand, and the instant I did, a flicker of warmth and other memories—shadows?—began to stir inside of me.

"All right." I barely registered my lips moving. "But what about Storm?"

"My other House Sister, Stella, can take over for you. I will tell the rest of my family I am going to take you to register as my choice for a House Mother."

My heart jumped excitedly. "You are?"

"Not right now."

"Oh." I pulled my hand free from his, brushing back my hair so he could not see my distress. "So you don't want me to be your House Mother?"

"You're so close. I know it's hard, but you have to fight it." Aidan came up next to me, so close my skirts were brushing up against his pants. He leaned over and pressed his lips against mine, and for a moment, nothing else ever seemed more real.

The moment began to flicker away even before that second was over, and my subconscious began to fight as the memory tried to leave.

No, let it stay. Let me keep this one.

I did not know who I was begging, or if there was anyone listening, but the power of my hidden self—that center of my being, the one at the core of every secret I'd kept from the world, and maybe even myself—won, and I fell into Aidan's arms a second later.

The taste of him, coupled with his embrace, felt more than familiar to me—less like a dream, and more like a dream come true. As he pulled back from me, my fingers curled around his sleeves.

"How many times have we done that before?" I asked.

"None. But I've been thinking about it for a long time."

My cheeks flushed. "You have?"

"Yes." He brushed back my hair, pressing a kiss on the side of my neck. It was just like that moment before, when I had imagined him brushing up from behind me, when I'd been washing out Storm's baby bottles. "I've thought about it, ever since I was fourteen and you asked me if I ever saw shadows in the early morning. Do you remember?"

No part of me could recall telling him about the shadows, but that was the moment when I knew he was telling me the truth.

At my silence, Aidan stepped back, letting me slide out of his arms as he nodded. "I had a feeling you'd forgotten," he said. "You only remember our talks when it's something that causes a strong, emotional reaction."

"I'm … " For a long moment, I stared at him, and I tried to form the words I wanted to say.

I'm sorry.

The old history books talked of the Imperfect Past, the time when there was a need for apologies, but I had never uttered the word with the full weight of its meaning behind it.

"There's something wrong here, Skyla, and you have to see it."

I nodded. "Okay."

As soon as I was able to drop Storm off with Aidan's sister, he took me by the hand and led me down to the Festival.

At the sights before me, my eyes widened with pleasure, my vision overflowing with happiness. The Festival was full of so many fun rides, there were animals ready to ride, and, oh, how the smell of baked goods wafted up from the different dessert ration stations!

It was perfection, and I was never so glad as I was in that moment that I would get to be a part of it.

The whole City Center, from the top of the tower by the shoreline to the fields of flowers that blended into the horizon, was ablaze with colorful, shiny happiness.

Off to the side, I saw River helping to put up a tent.

"River!" I called, waving furiously. "River, over here!"

Aidan grabbed my hand. "Stop it. We're not supposed to be here."

"Why not?" I asked. "There are plenty of others around. And you are supposed to be helping them get ready for the Learning Ceremony."

"You're not supposed to be here. And what I am about to show you is forbidden, too."

"What is it?"

He ducked around a hedge, one that was just outside the tower by the seashore. I followed close behind him, as quietly as I could. It was then that I felt the onslaught of pain and tiredness like never before, and the shard in my forehead seemed to pulsate with pressure.

I rubbed my head with my one hand, refusing to drop Aidan's hand as he pressed onward.

A few moments later, we reached the door to the inside of the tower. Aidan jiggled the lock and opened the door a crack, before he pulled back.

"This is the surprise for the new graduates," Aidan said, his shoulders rigid and his voice tense. "This is what you will see at the Learning Ceremony."

A sudden thrill raced through me, enough that I hardly noticed the stab of pain emanating from my shard.

"Really?"

Before Aidan could answer me, I raced inside the building, never stopping to realize the darkness inside.

"Skyla, wait," Aidan called from behind me.

But I didn't hear him. I heard *it* instead.

"No!"

Someone was screaming, crying out in pure, agonizing pain.

Instantly, my hands reached up and closed off the sound, but the shrieking was too pervasive. The wrenching echo of all-encompassing pain and suffering permeated my soul.

My eyes blurred with tears, but I could still see it.

I could see *him.*

A frail, childlike figure cowered in the center of the tower room. He was flooded with light that burned scarlet, as different stripes tore open on his skin. I looked on him in horror, but I was unable to take my gaze away from him. The boy wore only a small, swaddling cloth around his loins, and his feet were bare and covered in wounds and bruises of all sorts.

My stomach was queasy, and I nearly doubled over as I inched closer to him. As I watched, his eyes met mine.

A shard glowed on his forehead, just the same as mine, only his was a scorching red. As we stared at each other, my sickness went away, and a second later, the boy vomited all over himself.

"No," I whispered, grabbing my stomach.

The boy before me mimicked my movements, grabbing his stomach and slumping over.

My own pain evaporated again, and as I felt my body's wellness return, I glanced at his nose, shocked and appalled to see it was crooked and bleeding freely, as though it had broken quite recently.

"No," I whispered again, but I knew no matter how much I denied it, it was still the truth.

The boy groaned as a bruise appeared around his left eye, but he took a step toward me.

"Skyla." His voice called out to me inside my mind; I thought I saw his split lips form my name, but I heard no whisper of sound as he spoke. The boy's hand reached out for mine, palm facing up, the same way Aidan had come to retrieve me earlier.

I did not have any notion of how Aidan managed to tear me away from the boy, but the second he rescued me from that room, I broke down, crying uncontrollably, as I never had ever before.

I understood now. I was awake, truly awake, at last. Those dark moments I had sensed in the early hours of the morning—they were shadows of the future, and the present. That sensation was the reality of my daily life—the daily, imperfect life of humanity's curse that the wretched boy inside the tower experienced for me.

I curled my fingers into my palms, scraping for any remnant of courage I could possibly have inside of me.

"Skyla."

Aidan's voice was starkly quiet against the roar of rage brewing inside of me. I looked up and realized he had been holding me, letting me cry into his chest. His perfect white shirt was now wet. As I watched, my tears dissolved from the fabric, no doubt magicked away and given to the boy to experience. I shook my head, absolutely horrified all over again, as I looked on all the proof I needed.

My life was not perfect—it only *seemed* perfect, and it was all because my suffering was taken away and given to a child to experience. I gripped Aidan's shirt tightly, as if trying to keep my tears in place.

"I knew you were someone who could see," he said, running his hand down my back, trying to comfort me.

I found strength in Aidan's kindness. If he could see, too, then he knew we were both looking at the hard, damning truth of imperfection.

"This isn't right." I shook my head. "We have to do something."

"Yes."

There was a tenderness in the icy color of his eyes, a new sort of kindness I might never have seen before, or perhaps one I might have imagined never happened before the onset of summer.

As his hand tightened around mine, I spoke the only words I could find, the only words which offered me any chance of absolution and any hope despite my imperfection and despair.

"We have to fight."

± ± ± ±

THE ONES WHO FIGHT

PART TWO

± ± ± ±

I did not know how much time had passed while Aidan dragged me through the streets. He was kind enough to make sure no one saw me as I tried to stop crying.

I was grateful for Aidan's kindness and his thoughtfulness. My tears were dissolving as they escaped me, but I was sure I looked awful. All I could see as we walked was the boy and all the horror surrounding him.

No. This can't be true.

In my perfect life, living in the City by the Sea, there was a tower that gleamed with sunlight, its bricks white and bright, a pinnacle of brilliance striking out in the world. It was the tower where we gathered to celebrate throughout the year; it was the place that housed the Learning Ceremony, the Community's formal initiation into adulthood—

It's not a "perfect" life. Stop calling it that.

I'd been excited to go there, and even more happy to have Aidan by my side as he sneaked me into the tower.

But then I went inside.

Inside the tower was a young boy—a boy who was constantly tortured. A boy who was subjected to bear all my life's pains, everything from smaller inconveniences to larger agonies. He had, like all of the Community members, a shard in the middle of his forehead, one that glowed with constant suffering. As I had watched him through a layer of tears, he called out to me.

"Can you walk?" Aidan asked beside me.

I didn't answer him. How could I? He might have just rescued me from the tower, but the scene I'd witnessed relentlessly repeated itself in my mind. Sickened, I relived that moment of tragic discovery over and over and over again, and I had to steel myself against the oncoming ocean of inner torment.

Forcing myself to stop feeling was the only way I could stop the boy from taking my pain away from me. All of my life had been perfect, up until that moment, and it was all because of that boy.

There was another sudden surge of pain in my forehead, just below the jewel that rested in the middle of my brow. My fingers pressed into my temples, as I forced myself to breathe; as much as it pained me even more, I held onto the memories of the terror I'd seen, determined to see the small, frail boy before me, the one who bore the marks of my life's imperfection.

"Skyla."

Aidan's voice seemed to come from far away, and the world spun as my head snapped up, looking at him.

"Skyla, hold still. I can help," he said.

"No, no you can't," I whispered. "I saw what was happening in there. That boy. He's taking everything from us. He's suffering for us."

My eyes squeezed shut as another twinge of pain lanced through my forehead, this time more urgent and demanding than before.

"I need you to hold still," Aidan hissed, taking my cheeks between his hands. He stepped up next to me, letting the shard on his forehead scrape against mine. The pain terrorizing me—the one demanding I give up my memory—began to fade, lessened by the friction between Aidan's shard and mine.

"What are you doing?" I asked him quietly, opening my eyes to see his icy blue ones staring into mine.

"How are you feeling?" His voice was deceptively calm; his eyes were wild as I watched him. He was likely regretting his actions, or he was unsure that showing me the tower had been the right thing to do.

He seemed to realize there was no going back, though. A moment later, he pulled back and pressed into my shard, before twisting it.

"Ouch," I muttered, but a second later, I was surprised to see he'd managed to pull part of it out of my forehead.

"What is—what did you … ?" My mouth dropped open as I stared at the top of my shard, watching as it faded from the blue to a deep obsidian.

"At the Learning Ceremony, the Elders surrounded us, thanked us, and then one of them, Lady Sula, reached forward and touched the shard, pressing into it, almost as if she was adjusting it. Some of the other kids' shards came out, just like yours," Aidan explained. "After that, I wasn't able to forget things anymore, or at least, not as easily."

"That's so strange," I said. "What do you think it's made out of?"

"I don't know." He shrugged. "I especially wasn't able to forget about the boy. But I wasn't able to speak about it, either. Not freely."

"So the shard is controlling us?" I asked. I took the small jewel from Aidan. I'd always loved my shard. As I turned it over in my hand, I saw there were two small metal rods sticking out from the bottom, no doubt where they connected to the small divot in my forehead.

I touched my forehead, tenderly feeling the shard's setting; it felt round and smooth, but there was a humming quality to it, almost like a magnet. I did not have any further idea of what it truly was, or what kind of power it housed.

"I don't know if it controls us," Aidan admitted. "But it makes sense to me. I know from working that the Community Elders have access to some highly advanced technology. Let me see if I can adjust yours like they did mine."

With Aidan's help, I put the shard back in my forehead; for a moment, I took a quick inventory of myself, feeling only a queasy blend of fear and freedom at the loss of my ignorance. When it did not disappear, I grimaced; I did not like these, even if it was better knowing the boy did not suffer with my pain.

"How are you?" Aidan asked.

"Terrible," I admitted with a half-smile. "But I have to say, I don't know if this is technology. There's something about it that still has an unreal quality to it."

I pressed my finger down onto the shard again, surprised to feel a sense of overwhelming contentment drip onto me. It didn't seem quite right to me, the idea of technology transferring all my pain to someone else for their full experience. And for me to feel something else instead? It all seemed too preposterous for words.

But there were things I did know for sure now, including the suffering boy in the tower by the sea.

"Your guess is as good as mine as to what it is, exactly."

I gave Aidan a trembling smile. "We don't have the luxury of guesses anymore, do we?"

"We always have time to remain complacent," Aidan said, his voice resigned.

I scowled. "Well, now we have to do something about this, Aidan. It's not right what they're doing in there. They're making a small, innocent boy take on all our pain and suffering."

"I know," Aidan said, his voice edged with regret and impatience. "I've known for a year now."

"Why haven't you done anything before this?" I asked, suddenly curious. Why would Aidan—someone I trusted more than I'd realized—allow someone to suffer wrongly for so long?

"Skyla … " He sighed. "It's very hard to leave the City by the Sea."

"After seeing what they do?" I frowned this time, indignation settling inside my heart. I wanted to leave right at that moment and never look back. My eyes welled up with tears at the mere thought of that lonely boy, the one surrounded by terror, the one who took all my trouble away. "How could you stay?"

"You know why, Skyla. My whole life is here," Aidan whispered. "And so is yours. You have your House Mother, your House Father, River, and all of your friends, just as I have mine. They're here, and all of the people who are here have chosen to stay here."

That was true.

"Our lives are happy, even if we know that it's because of something that's beyond terrible," Aidan said.

Some part of my memory chimed at Aidan's familiar words, and I was ashamed to recall that I'd had similar thoughts. Aidan had stayed for the very reasons I'd thought leaving was impossible.

But …

"But that doesn't make it right!" I yelped, and Aidan put a finger to my lips.

"What good would it do, for me to walk away?" he asked, his voice a low whisper between us. "The boy would still suffer if I left, and I would suffer, too. Many people stay because this place is part of who we are, and we don't want to leave the people here we love."

His eyes softened as he looked at me again. The clear blue of his irises pierced into my soul, and I realized why he wanted to stay. A raging fire burned within me all of a sudden, the flame hot and urgent as it sent tingles through my whole body before the heart of it settled, curling around inside of my belly.

"I love you," Aidan whispered. "There are a lot of moments of my life where I feel as though I am waking up from a dream, as though I am forgetting something important and I need to lose myself again if I am going to find it. But when I see you, I know I am home."

He stepped even closer to me and took hold of my hands. "I am not going to leave my home, Skyla."

I squeezed his hands back. If I was his anchor to reality, he was my reason for hope. He might have stayed behind in the City by the Sea, with all its hidden darkness, but he did not agree with it.

And that meant it was possible we could do something about it.

I took a step closer to Aidan, pressing my shard up against his. Even though I could not see it, I knew it was burning bright pink; I could feel the rush of affection for him. The deep roots of my love, perhaps lost in all the memories I'd had wiped away or altered, were firm, and I could feel the flower of my love for him blossom.

The sublime beauty of that moment was contrasted sharply with the reality we now faced.

"We have to fight this," I said quietly.

"I know." Aidan's voice, this close to me, reverberated against my skin. I shivered at the sensation, even though I was warmed by his certainty.

"What are we going to do?"

"I don't know." Aidan sighed. "But we'll think of something. If nothing else, I am glad you know. For now, you need to get ready for the Learning Ceremony. I know I am supposed to be helping there, too."

He backed away from me, letting his hands slide from mine as slowly as possible. Affection between friends was encouraged in the City by the Sea, but I had a feeling a number of people would be disconcerted by the blazing passion I saw in Aidan's eyes as we finally let each other go.

"Promise me you won't forget this."

I blinked, appalled he would even suggest it, but, as I recalled how I'd forgotten so much of his kindness and attention before, I clenched my fist, feeling more determined than ever. My nails dug into my palms, and at the pain, I paused as my shard seemed to hum softly.

"I won't forget this," I said, uncurling my fists.

I did not want to hurt the boy anymore. I didn't feel my pain leaving me, but I was not sure if he would receive it or not. I did know that I would remember the boy, just as I would remember Aidan's love—no matter the cost.

I made my silent vow as Aidan and I faced our street, where our two houses were in line with all the others.

"Aidan."

"What is it?"

"When I was thirteen, and I asked you about the shadows in the morning, what did you tell me?"

He looked over at me. "I don't remember it all, to be honest. It's one of the first things I remember on my own, without it being taken from me. But I remember telling you not to tell anyone else, and that they would see it as an overactive imagination."

I nodded slowly. "I thought that myself. That's why I never told anyone but you, I think."

"That's the first day I decided I liked you," Aidan said.

I reveled in that feeling of bedazzlement, before the shard in my forehead began to buzz; I could hear it this time; I could feel it changing colors as I looked at Aidan.

A sudden thought struck me as we approached our houses.

"Do you think people would remember their pain and their other memories better if we freed the boy?"

"Where would we take him?" Aidan asked. "The Community Elders might be away today, but there aren't a lot of openings for breaking him free. I might have tried that myself, if I thought it would work."

Aidan told me all about his moments of planning, about the pitfalls of each of his plans. As he escorted me to the door of my house, his voice fell into silence, as if he was aware that mourning over his failure would be frowned upon by others.

"I love you even more for all of this, you know," I told him, as I knocked on the door and waited for my House Mother or Father to open it. "You're a good person, Aidan, for telling me and helping me. And wanting to do something."

"It doesn't matter what I thought," Aidan said, shaking his head. "I didn't do anything."

"You helped me." I took his hand again, unwilling to let him go.

Before he could say anything else, the door opened up, and we were immediately surrounded by our families.

"There they are!"

Aidan and I jumped in surprise at Aidan's sister, Stella, as she announced our arrival. Our collective house members—Mother Annika and Mother Erika, our House Fathers, Stella and even Storm—all of them stood in the door before us.

Uneasiness crept into me, before it slipped away into uncertain happiness.

"You should have told everyone you were going to ask Skyla to be your House Mother," Stella said, bouncing a cheery Storm on her hip. "We could have had more time to prepare something for you!"

"Prepare?" Aidan asked.

"For your Joining Ceremony. Come in, and we can celebrate until it is time to go to the Summer Festival."

We were pulled inside and pushed around, everyone alternatively offered me advice and congratulations; I vaguely recalled Aidan had told Stella he was going to take me as his House Mother, and that meant there was a lot that went with it. Before we were separated by the different parties, Aidan and I exchanged a knowing glance.

It was almost as if I could hear his thoughts.

They don't know. They won't help.

Before I knew it, I was telling them of how Aidan and I planned to move closer to the tower, how we wanted to start a family of our own, how we would apply for Child Rearing as soon as we were able. And when Mother Annika said there was a waiting time of at least four years for a new baby, I assured her that it was the perfect amount of time to wait for such a joy.

Stella handed me a piece of cake, and Mother Erika gave me a kiss on the cheek, welcoming me to her House Son's family. Aidan's House Father, Robert, shook my hand and began to sing a song of joy and celebration.

It was while he began to sing that I somehow heard River's voice through the crowd.

"You're just asking for trouble, joining with her," he sneered.

The singing faded into the background, and my eyes shifted over just in time to see Aidan's gaze frost over, and he hit River across the face.

River doubled over, nearly falling to the ground before he was righted, and the blood on his lip was replaced by a wholesome smile.

I almost forgot the charade for the second, wanting to yell at both River and Aidan, but I stopped myself—though only barely.

Thankfully, no one else noticed what happened.

And that's when the idea began to form inside my mind.

"I'm so happy for you both," Mother Annika said, brushing a lock of hair from my face. "You will make an excellent House Mother for Aidan, Skyla."

"Yes, Storm is always happy to see you," Mother Erika agreed.

"I would love to have a child," I said, suddenly thinking of all the daydreams I was now allowed to have, since I was supposedly a House Mother. I could see Aidan and me as we worked together, keeping house and attending to our jobs. We would have two children to start, and then when they were older, if we had fulfilled our task well enough, we would be given another one or two. All

House Parents had children for as long as possible, until the youngest from each family took care of us in our later years, until we were sixty.

The smile fled from my face at the thought.

Sixty years of torturing that boy. All for a perfect life.

I shook my head.

If Aidan and I were going to fight, the first thing we would have to do was free him.

"What is it, Skyla?" Mother Annika asked. "You are not smiling."

I cleared my throat carefully, after feeling the sharp spike behind the shard on my forehead. "I am well." I forced myself to smile. "I am … thinking of where we will live now."

"Oh, do not even think about that," Erika said. "The Community will decide what is best for you, just like they do for everyone else."

I felt my teeth grind against each other as I nodded, all while the image of the boy, being tortured with all the pain of the Community members, raced through my mind.

A bell chimed in the distance, marking the opening call for the Summer Festival, and both relief and sadness coursed through me. For now, I would have to lay my dreams of a life with Aidan aside. Perhaps I would have to do it forever, and that thought made my heart ache even more than the shard in my forehead did.

Aidan tugged on me, pulling me out from my oncoming despair.

"Come on, Sky," he said. "Let's go to the Festival."

"Yes," Mother Annika said. "Skyla might be your choice for a House Mother, but she still has to complete the Learning Ceremony."

± ± ± ±

Time did not seem to pass at all while we walked towards the tower. There were more stations set up since I had been there last, or maybe I just noticed them more, taking them in with a bland eye.

It was when I caught the sight of the oceanfront that the rest of my plan came together in my mind, and I squeezed Aidan's hand at once.

"What is it?" he asked.

Out of the corner of my eye, I noticed he was looking at me, letting his gaze take in my dress and the twisted flowers in my hair. Another wave of warmth, one that had nothing to do with the weather, washed through me. I almost forgot what I was going to say when he asked me, "Is something bothering you?"

I sighed, then whispered, "I have been thinking. If the shard is what controls us, we should free that boy and take his shard. If we can dismantle it, he should be saved from the pain other people experience."

"The Community Elders will not like that."

"No," I agreed. "They will not be for it at all. That's why I need you to distract them somehow."

"Distract them?" Aidan frowned. "How?"

"I don't know," I admitted. "But no one in my house saw you punch River when he was being … rude … about us."

It had taken me a moment to recall the word, but the moment I said it was the moment I knew it was the right one.

"I don't know if I'll be able to think of something."

"You thought of telling your sister you were going to ask me to be your House Mother," I reminded him. "Because of that, everyone else in our Houses was distracted and didn't see you."

"You did," Aidan pointed out.

"We've already established that we are the ones who can see certain things others can't," I said. "It makes sense I saw it, even if the others didn't. Just try to think of something else, something that will distract them. Something that's not bad enough to be erased, but something that will cause people to look at you for a few moments."

Aidan hesitated, but then he nodded. "All right. But you'll have to work quickly."

"I'll free the boy, and then I'll take him down to the caves we used to play in as kids," I said, looking back toward the oceanfront.

The boy was malnourished and thin which made the punishments he received all the more terrible. But there was hope in that, I decided. He wouldn't be too heavy, and I would be able to get him out of the tower long enough to get the shard out of his forehead.

"Skyla."

Aidan dropped my hand as Lady Sula's voice called out for me.

Carefully, with a bright smile, I turned around to face her. "Lady Sula," I said, giving her a small curtsey. "How are you today?"

"I am well, Skyla."

Lady Sula had been the Lead Elder of my Community for as long as I could remember. She never seemed to age, but if I had to guess by looking at her, she was nearing her sixtieth year. Her long hair was pure white, and the shard in her head burned with total control all the time; every time I saw her, each of the seven rainbow colors evenly divided up the small gem, marking her as an Elder.

Her demeanor seemed to solidify the rest of her title. Despite her age, she stood straight, while other Elders were a little hunched. Her eyes, a perfect gray, were clear and alert. She had no wrinkles in her smile as she looked at me, and her gnarled hands seemed strong and firm despite the small splatter of gray freckles across her knuckles.

"I heard you will be a House Mother," Lady Sula said.

"Yes," I agreed, trying to look contrite and content at the same time.

"I did not see your registration," she continued. "You must go down to the Elders' Housing after the Learning Ceremony to correct this oversight."

Aidan stepped forward. "It was my overexcitement," he said. "I will fix it."

"You will both need to go," Lady Sula said. "And Aidan, remember your manners. We live in a perfect world, and we make it all the more beautiful when we remember how fragile that beauty is."

She gave us a quick nod, smiled, and then walked away, taking her place at the entrance to the tower.

Aiden tugged my hand again. "I'm going to go in and find your brother," he said. "As a member of last year's class, I am allowed to go and stand with this year's graduates. They will do some introductions before showing everyone the boy. In the meantime, you go see if you can sneak around and find him."

"All right." I swallowed hard, and Aidan leaned over and gave me a quick, stolen kiss on the cheek before he left me.

I felt each footstep he took as though it was a stomp on my heart. I could only hope that the boy did not feel all of my pain, now that Aidan had fiddled with my shard; if so, I wondered if my sudden sorrow at his parting might kill him.

There were a few ways into the tower, and I quickly spotted an entrance as I joined the adults heading into the tower. It was a small building, but the Community was not all here yet.

It made me sick to think of how each year I would have to witness the boy getting beaten and barraged by my pain.

A worse thought hit me as I slunk my way around the hidden hallways of the tower: What if someone actually enjoyed watching the boy suffer, and deliberately set out to cause him even more pain?

I did not want to think about that. Such cruelty did not seem possible.

And yet it was, wasn't it?

That was the reason for the Imperfect Times. That was the reason that we were all here, forcing a young boy to take on all our pain and troubles. We ourselves were capable of all those things—hurting others, hurting ourselves, falling into the harshest cruelties of the human heart.

"Welcome to the 83rd Annual Summer Festival!"

A Elder's voice called out through the tower, and I nearly screamed at the sudden, booming voice. I held my hand over my mouth to stop myself from making any noise, and it had to be a matter of divine providence that I did, because in that very next second, my shard began to buzz, vibrating with pain and sorrow.

Tears filled my eyes, as if to prepare me.

He's near.

Another layer of pain struck me hard and fast, the same as it had before, when I'd first seen the boy.

I was getting closer.

A doorway on my left glowed with crimson fire, and—with a new surge of anguish pouring into my forehead—I opened it.

There he was. The same boy as before.

His eyes met mine as I stepped inside the room.

"I knew it was you, Skyla."

The voiceless whisper in my head spoke, without his chapped and broken lips moving.

Before I could tell him I was there to rescue him, I realized the room's ceiling was made of thick glass. The light was flooding all around him, and I could see a new cut form with a line of blood on his arm as I came closer.

If I had been in the Learning Ceremony line, like I was supposed to be, I would have only seen the lights. There were lines up above, and I knew that they would open up, showcasing the boy's torment for all to see.

Through the glass, I could see Lady Sula was reigning over the room. I could hear her talking about the Learning Ceremony, and how good it was that we had all made it to this moment of our lives.

"Now," she called out to the young people in the crowd, "now you will know the truth that comes with the Age of Accountability, and you must face your choice: Will you stay in the City by the Sea, or will you leave us?"

There was a loud chorus of naysayers, those who already were determined to stay. Had I not known the truth, I might have been among them.

But then I thought about being Aidan's House Mother, about holding a child we were to raise; I imagined working at a job I loved, every day, no matter what it was; I thought about getting to kiss Aidan in our own house, whenever I wanted, in the years before we would be eligible for Child Rearing.

Maybe I would be one of the naysayers, too, even if I knew the truth. If I was not down here …

I squeezed my eyes shut in pain, angered and frustrated. All my life I had been told I was good, but in that moment, when I truly knew what good was, I knew I was not.

I would have been happy, I would have been content, I would have been productive, and I even would have been loving and kind to others. But I would not have been good.

"It's all right, you know."

"What?" I opened my eyes.

The boy in the center of the room was now before me, and his gaze had never left my face. I realized he had been able to read my thoughts.

"It's all right for you to want a good life," he said.

"But it's not good for you to pay the price for me to do that." I shook my head. "I don't even know your name. Who are you?"

"My name is Ai," he said, in that strange, voiceless tone. It was louder than a whisper in my head this time.

"Ai. It's nice to meet you," I whispered back, before I held out my hand to him.

The scarlet chains of light surrounding him scorched my palm, but I did not stop reaching for Ai. It was something I had to suffer for—honestly, truly suffer for—and after my life of perfection, it was the smallest amount of sacrifice I could give.

And even while the light burned into my flesh, making my tears swell and augment, I felt a rush of joy inside of me. I knew I was doing the right thing.

As if to agree, just as I was about to grab Ai's hand, I heard Aidan's voice speak up above us.

"My Community," he said, racing into the center of the tower auditorium. "My Community, I ask of you to celebrate with me today, for I have chosen a House Mother!"

"Aidan Aeros." Lady Sula's voice cut through his, stopping his impromptu speech.

"Yes, Lady Sula, it is me," he agreed, doing his best to play off her words as a sign of reassurance, rather than discouragement. "I wanted to let the Community know I have asked for Skyla Mercer's hand today, to join in mine as a House Mother."

Ai smiled crookedly at me. "He is a good man."

"I know," I whispered back, before I grabbed his hand.

The next few moments were blurry to me, as my hand wrapped around his. The light around us changed, darkening the room around us as well as the one above us.

From what I could see, there were more people paying attention to Aidan, as he gushed about his love for me and all my goodness. It pained me that I had to run away, and even more so when I realized Ai was not helping.

"What are you doing?" Ai gasped and, as we left the room, the rest of the tower went dark.

"Getting you out of here," I said. I did not have time to wonder if there was any other course of action. I simply picked him up, horrified at his lightness, and hurried out.

Ai struggled against me, all the way down to the caves. Behind us, I could hear Lady Sula and the other Elders, calling out in horror, some of them telling the audience to remain still while they sought to find a way to "better" their "unexpected situation." I swore I could have heard the faintest strain of fear in Lady Sula's voice as I ducked into the caves down by the seafront.

It was then, in the summer's diminishing sunlight, that I saw Ai's mouth move and form words.

"What have you done?"

His voice was choked and cracked, and immediately my motherly instincts cradled him against my breast.

"I've saved you," I said, unable to stop some of my tears from falling on his cheek.

Ai pulled back from me, looking up at me in horror. He used one crooked, scraped finger to touch the shard on his forehead, and I could see his eyes grow wide as he realized he was no longer receiving any pain or experiencing the heartache of any Community member.

"*We* saved you," I said, this time thinking of Aidan. I did not want to bruise Ai's body further, but I reached out and hugged him tightly again. I embraced him, in part as an apology for all the pain of mine he'd taken away over the years. "I'm sorry about everything. But you're safe now. Everything will be alright now."

The boy eased back from me. "No," he said.

"What?" I blinked in shock and stepped away. "What are you talking about? You're *innocent.* You shouldn't have to suffer because of the rest of us."

"This is the covenant of the Bloodmagic," Ai whispered. "As long as there is life and sin, there will be suffering. Over the centuries, different groups have tried to find a way to eliminate it, but it is impossible. So one life takes on all suffering."

"But … but that's not fair!" My mouth dropped open, as I watched him.

"It might not seem fair to you, but those are the terms, Skyla. If you do not return me to the tower now, you will see. Bloodmagic runs deep, and now that you've saved me, I fear you've condemned us all."

± ± ± ±

THE ONES WHO CHOOSE

PART THREE

± ± ± ±

± ± ± ±

It was past nightfall as I ran through the City by the Sea. After the sun went down and the night only offered starlight, I'd left Ai in the seaside caves with Aidan.

Now I was trying to outrun my fear and hoping against hope there was something better to run toward.

"I fear you've condemned us all."

The words, so stark and hopeless, slapped through my mind, again and again, pulling at the pain in my heart.

The harshness of the air, strangely full of ash and mist, beat into my mouth as I panted, setting my lungs on fire. There was a storm coming, and I instinctively knew it would be much worse than the usual ones we had in our seaside town.

"Ouch," I whimpered, rubbing the back of my hand against my forehead. The shard I'd had placed there since my birth buzzed with frightful anger, and I didn't know if it was because I was feeling it myself, or if the Community thought I was supposed to feel it.

A gash of lightning struck across the skies, and at the resounding, thunderous clap that crashed in time with the flicker of lights, I stumbled and fell. My knee scraped against the ground, and I could feel the sting of blood rushing out of my bruised skin.

No one took away my pain this time.

I sobbed, the sound jarring against the ominous darkness of the oncoming storm. Endless questions about my pain, and why I deserved it, and how this could happen, and how I was going to ever recover from this—all of these questions overwhelmed me and left me crying louder.

Is this because of Ai?

At the thought of the boy Aidan and I had rescued, I started to calm down. My tears slowed instead of disappearing, and I took several deep, gulping breaths as I sat on the ground, clutching my blood-covered knee, moping over my injury as much as the damage to my new dress. The white lacy fabric absorbed the scarlet of my blood as quickly as the lightning shot through the sky, and it was a long moment that I sat there, mourning.

Despite all of that foreign pain and dread, it was nothing when compared to the truth.

I suffered now because of my own actions, instead of those consequences being transferred to Ai, the small boy my Community had tortured for an unknown time, using him and strange technology and something Ai referred to as "Bloodmagic" to absorb all of the Community's ills.

At that thought, I touched the shard on my forehead again, and as my fingertips grazed it, it began to hum almost angrily.

There was a shard on Ai's forehead, too, one I'd seen grow bloody red with pain and suffering. I nearly doubled over as I recalled the first time I saw him. My stomach heaved with a stitch in my side, and I nearly cried out, fearing the worst at the sudden sickness.

After an easy life of perfection, only understanding the Imperfect Past as stories and facts about humanity's previous times, I was not used to suffering from my own pain.

I hated feeling weak, even more than I hated feeling helpless.

I struggled to stand, positioning myself against the wind and storm, as I limped forward, heading for my home.

Together with Aidan—the one who loved me, the one who'd lived next to me all my life—I had freed Ai from his captivity in the tower, the one where the City by the Sea had come to celebrate the Summer Festival and the Learning Ceremony. It was the very ceremony where we were inducted into the Community as full members, if we decided to stay in the city. If we wanted to leave, we were granted that right.

Thanks to Aidan's distraction, I'd been able to take the wounded, malnourished boy to the caves down by the oceanfront. Several hours had passed since his rescue, and I needed to go and get something to help Ai with all his sustained injuries.

After all those years of experiencing such pain, Ai was badly injured, suffering, and he told me it was only because of Bloodmagic that he was alive. Now that he was free of the Community's prison, the bond he had with the Bloodmagic was weakening, and if I didn't help him, he would die.

I have to get home.

Death—something only the Elders in my Community ever oversaw—propelled me forward like nothing else.

I had to help Ai. After all he had suffered, it was the least I could do.

I needed my sewing kit, maybe some of my older clothes to use as bandages; if I could find anything for him to eat, that might help, too. Of course, even if I did have something that could help heal him entirely, I didn't know if it would be enough to help with the Bloodmagic Ai told me about.

I slowed to a stop, as I finally spotted my house. It was brightly lit, the windows pouring out light, but even from where I was, I could hear my House Mother and House Father fighting; upstairs, River was in his room, yelling at both of them to shut up and smashing the glass out of the window panes.

Ai's earlier warning about Bloodmagic came back to me, strong and certain.

"He wasn't lying," I whispered, nearly choking on the words. "This is terrible."

± ± ± ±

Before I'd left to return home, Ai started talking to me about the Bloodmagic.

After I'd rescued him from the tower, I had taken him down to the caves. I'd settled him in one as best as I could, and then faced the cave entrance, keeping a lookout for Aiden. I was more concerned for Aidan at first; I didn't know if he was coming or not. There was a good chance that when Ai was taken, the Community Elders would find a way to keep everyone in the tower until they had answers. As much as we were both in this together, I didn't know what to expect now that we'd accomplished something this big.

But as Ai kept talking to me, and considering his talk of condemnation, I began to ask Ai questions. It didn't take us long to talk about Bloodmagic.

"Bloodmagic is their word for the sacrifice," Ai said.

"What?" My head snapped to look at him, as if to make sure he wasn't trying to fool me. Instantly, I regretted my action, seeing his mangled body and the sad condition it was in. That was part of the reason I'd offered to stand watch in the caves, keeping my focus on the entrance. While I did not want the

Community Elders to find us, and although I was watching for Aidan, I did not want to look at Ai roo much. He made me feel uncomfortable.

Ai slumped beside me, looking out toward the cave entrance. The last of the sunlight was gone, and the temperature dropped. Ai did not seem to notice, even if he was nearly naked, with only a thin cloth around his loins.

"They call humanity's curse 'Bloodmagic,'" Ai said. "That is their name for it. I don't think they like to think about it much."

"If this is why you've been hurt, they probably don't like to think of it," I said. I glanced at him quickly, before reverting my eyes back to the cave entrance. "This is terrible."

"It is," Ai agreed. "But it is like I told you before. All of my suffering is your suffering."

"That's not right."

He shook his head. "It doesn't matter. I have been alive for nearly a century, thanks to the Bloodmagic, and this is just the way things are. That is why I would prefer that you return me to my tower room."

"What?" I gasped at the remark. "No. Why would you want that?"

"The Community won't survive long, Skyla," Ai said. "Without the Bloodmagic Covenant, the full effects of suffering will return to your friends and family swiftly and mercilessly. They will suffer, and in their suffering, they will make others suffer more. They might even begin to enjoy hurting others if we don't hurry."

"But *you* will suffer if you return," I said. "And I will make you suffer, too. I don't want that. Can't something else be done about the Bloodmagic?"

"There is nothing that can be done about human nature," Ai said quietly. "We are prone to self-destruction, and we live in a world where pain and suffering are constants. All the countries and nations of the world have wrestled with this question, and in the end, all of the pain still exists. Many tried to fix the problem and only made it worse.

"So they decided to try something else. And it works." He reached up and touched the shard on his forehead, the one what was darkening along with the sky. "If I am not returned, the suffering will only increase, and you will see people at their very worst. Every evil, selfish, and ignorant thought will manifest into danger and disaster. I've been able to hold off their degeneracy for a long time, and without me, they will exponentially become violent and careless."

"Surely we still have some more time to stop them." I put my hands together, trying to think of something else. "Maybe it is a matter of education. The adults here are smart.

They'll be able learn how to deal with the pains our Community has."

Ai shook his head. "You don't understand," he said with a sad sigh. "But you will, once you see it. You must promise me you will not forget me when you do, or you could be at risk, too."

From that moment, we lapsed into silence, and I was grateful.

I shivered as we sat there, but I didn't think it was because of the chill in the air.

± ± ± ±

I began to understand what Ai had meant as I opened the door to my house.

Mother Annika, my House Mother, was wailing as she moved about the kitchen, where earlier that day, she'd been busy baking for the Summer Festival.

"My pies," she cried, pulling a smoking bundle out of the oven. I could smell the burnt peaches wafting up, filling the room as she whirled around and faced my House Father.

"What are you whining about now, woman?" My House Father, Albert, was even louder than Mother Annika, but he was clearly more angry than anything else. "I told you to shut your mouth, and if you were smart, you'd never open it again. After everything that's happened today, I need peace and quiet!"

"I didn't hear the oven's timer go off because all you've been doing is yelling!" Mother Annika threw her burning pie onto the floor. It smashed, sending mushy peaches all over the kitchen. "For a man who needs peace and quiet, you sure don't like to shut up yourself!"

"You both need to shut up," River yelled from upstairs. "It's nighttime, and I want to go to sleep. This is why you're both terrible parents, and I hate you!"

I bit my lip, trying to swallow my whimper. Father Albert had always been so soft-spoken, so kind and generous. Hearing him yell was enough to make me want to run and hide, and I could only squeeze my eyes shut against the terror I faced from those around me. They were my family, but I did not recognize them.

It was only the thought of Ai suffering and Aidan depending on me that allowed me to ignore it and slip inside.

Immediately, I regretted it.

"Oh, look who's home at last," Father Albert said. "And just where were you, Skyla?"

"I was … around," I said, feeling guilty at the lie, even if I felt it was necessary.

"Were you with Aidan?" Father Albert scoffed. "If you want to keep him interested in you for a House Mother, you really should watch how much time you spend with him."

"Yes," Mother Annika agreed. "It's better to scare him off early, before the contract is final. Or you'll get stuck with a loser like Albert for a House Father."

"Who is the loser here?" Father Albert snapped back. "You can't even bake pies right. Erika's the best pie baker in the Community. I could have had her for a House Mother instead of you!"

"If you want pie, I'll give you some pie!" Mother Annika screamed back, and while she bent down and began to fling pie remnants at Father Albert, I fled to the stairs.

I had just placed my foot on the top floor when I heard a *smack!*

My hand went over my mouth as the sound repeated itself, and Mother Annika began to scream. Tears welled up in my eyes, as I realized what was happening. My House Father began to berate her as he hit her, condemning her for her ingratitude and her insolence.

This has to stop.

Before I could yell at them, River came out of his room.

His eyes were hard as they met mine. "Oh, there you are," he said. "Aidan's newest plaything, I guess. Perhaps I should offer you my congratulations, but I feel more obliged to give him my sympathies."

"Don't talk to me." My voice was hoarse as I hurried past him, heading for my room. I needed my sewing kit, I reminded myself, and then I could leave. I could leave and go back to Aidan.

If he was still himself, too.

"Aidan's too good for you," River scoffed, following me into my room. "I don't know what he was thinking. You're nothing special."

I ignored him as I grabbed my sewing kit. Remembering the coolness of the cave, I took my jacket as well.

"Maybe he's dumber than I thought," River said. "It never occurred to me that he would be stupid enough to pick you as a House Partner. Or maybe he thought it would be better to have a stupid House Mother, so he wouldn't have a hard time telling you what to do."

"Aidan's not stupid," I snapped. After all the years of finding my frustrations taken away before they could take root and come to fruition, a new sense of freedom ran through me as I faced River. "You're the stupid one, if you can't see I don't want to talk to you."

River snarled. "We'll see who's stupid," he said, and then he tried to punch me.

I ducked and hurried out of my room, slamming the door behind me. I winced as River pounded on it and hoped I would be able to keep him back.

"Let me out, Skyla!" I heard him walk away and then run for the door: he planned to crash into it and push me aside.

I opened the door at the last moment, letting him tumble through the doorway. He tripped and rolled, before smashing into the wall across from me.

River howled in pain, his forehead bleeding. I watched as the shard on his forehead began to buzz, screeching out a horrific noise as blood dripped down over it.

That feeling of self-righteousness came over me again, and I clenched my fists, trying to stop myself from making the situation worse.

Think of Ai. Think of Aidan. Don't do this to yourself … even if River deserves it.

I took a deep breath and hurried off, making sure to grab what I'd come for. River was still screaming, though now he was cursing me; downstairs, I could hear Mother Annika whimpering as Father Albert gathered his own belongings. He was yelling at her, telling her he'd had enough, and he was leaving the family.

I didn't know where he was going, but as he came out of their shared room, I knew I did not want to get in his way.

Once I was free of my house—would I ever be able to call it my home, ever again?—I took a deep breath, trying to keep calm.

I could still hear the noise coming from my house, but it was muffled, and I was grateful for the small defense.

That was before Erika opened the door to her house, carrying a bawling Storm. I was about to ask her what was wrong with the baby, before I remembered.

In freeing Ai, all of Storm's pain and suffering was now stuck with her, and that meant she would be in distress.

"Oh, by the Elders, stop it," Erika yelled at Storm. She saw me and breathed a sigh of relief. "Oh, Skyla, I'm glad you're here. I need you to take Storm away from me. She's already driven Stella from the house."

Storm was still wailing, wriggling as she screamed.

"I don't think I can take her," I started to say, before Erika began to shake her.

"Just … stop … crying!" Erika huffed, as Storm began to scream even harder.

Storm screamed louder, and I felt my heart break at her mother's carelessness.

"Stop," I said, stepping forward. "No, wait, I'll take her! Please, just don't—"

There was an ominous *snap*, loud enough that even the arguing from my own house behind me couldn't drown it out.

Storm went limp. Erika didn't seem to notice as she handed her roughly to me.

"Well, it's about time she stopped," Erika huffed. "Just take her for a bit for me, would you? Now that the Summer Festival is over, I need to clean up my house and go over my pie recipes."

"Mother Erika … I think she's dead." I was barely able to say anything as I held Storm in my hands. I tightened my hands around the tiny body and clutched her to my chest, trembling. I nearly fell over as I stared down at her. Storm's silence, coupled with her wet eyes and pliant limbs, was unnerving, and I was paralyzed.

I fear you've condemned us all.

Ai's words echoed hauntingly in my mind, and I nearly choked as I tried to cry.

"You shouldn't tell jokes like that, Skyla," Erika chastised me. "At this point, I'm too old to be a mother. I need to focus on my career, and I can't do it with a kid hanging around all the time. Just take her and take care of her for me for a few days. I need to work more, and you can think of this as a good practice run for when you apply for children for the Community."

I watched as Erika, relieved to be rid of Storm, headed back into her house without a second thought to her dead baby.

I cradled Storm's body, pressing her forehead to mine, letting my shard scratch her now-darkened one. "What have I done?" I whispered.

A thundering noise struck out against the night.

I held onto Storm, and the earlier pain in my knee as well as the anger I felt at River disappeared as I walked. I didn't know what else to do, but to return to the caves. Things were getting bad, and I didn't want to be around when they got worse.

I was nearly to the tower when I realized it was already worse.

The tower was lit up, surrounded by bright lights. The Community Elders were gathered around the tower, and they were holding onto long sticks of metal and wood …

My head began to swim with sickness as I recognized the objects.

Guns.

They were using them to fight back the crowds of angry people.

"We must have order!" Lady Sula's voice was grave and grizzly as she stood there, in the center.

I blinked and squinted at her.

I'd been so busy being shocked by the guns, I hadn't realized that I nearly didn't recognize Lady Sula.

Her face was full of wrinkles, and her hair, once a smooth and shining white waterfall behind her, was curled into white and gray wisps. It seemed as though several bunches of it were falling out as she stood there. She was hunched over, and her fingers were slower to move as she pointed and directed others around her.

An involuntary squeak escaped my lips; at the sound, I seemed to remember myself, and I hurried toward the caves. I ran, still limping slightly at the pain on my knee, still cradling Storm.

"Aidan." I called out to him as I approached the caves.

"Skyla."

There was nothing more wondrous to me than hearing him call my name.

I rushed over and embraced him. Even in the dark, I could see the lightness of his hair against the darkness of the night.

"What happened?" Aidan asked, as he looked down at Storm. Even in the dim light, I could see the horrified sadness as he realized the truth.

"I'm … " *Sorry.*

I barely remembered the word as Aidan took his baby sister in his arms.

"Your House Mother was shaking her," I said slowly. "I wasn't able to stop her in time."

Aidan was speechless as he held her, giving her a small kiss on her forehead.

"I warned you," Ai said behind us. "The people in the City by the Sea aren't accustomed to pain or handling the harder things of life."

"Aidan and I are still mostly fine," I lied, thinking of how much I'd enjoyed lashing out at River while trying to ignore the still-bleeding gash on my knee.

"You've dismantled your shard before, and you had some time to prepare yourself for this," Ai said, pointing to my forehead. "Even before then, you knew, didn't you, Skyla? You remember the shadows in the morning, don't you? You remember the memories of things that never really happened."

Ai was right. I'd felt something strange and otherworldly about the world before, and now I knew what it was: it was the shadows we carried inside of ourselves, the things we could never separate from who we were.

I looked down at my hands, remembering how they held Storm. All I felt was numb.

"The rest of the Community is not so lucky," Ai said. "They will lash out, fast and hard, and even the Elders won't be able to rein them in. You must return me to the tower."

Darkness grew, pressing in on me and pressing through me.

"This is bad, Aidan," I whispered. "Perhaps Ai is right."

"*This* is not right," Aidan replied, holding onto Storm. "Returning Ai will not solve the problem, Skyla. It will only mask the pain."

"He says it's nothing we can stop, thanks to the Bloodmagic," I objected. "It's not fair, but there's really nothing we can do about it, is there?"

Before Aidan and I could think through our options, a bright light shined on us from the cave entrance.

"There you are." Lady Sula's voice was scraggly now, much harsher than before. It seemed she was dwindling fast. "Traitors."

"We're not traitors," I yelled back. "We only wanted to do the right thing."

"You wanted to send this town into a circle of Hell?"

I frowned at her words, but several guards came at us, and before I knew it, Ai, Aidan, and I were all surrounded.

"Give me that," Lady Sula said, grabbing Storm out of Aidan's arms.

I did not want to know what she was going to do with her, but before I could find a way to ask anyway, we were marched up to the tower, away from the caves.

"Take the boy," Lady Sula barked. "Put him back in the tower so we can get the Community back together."

"This isn't fair," I said. "He's innocent."

"And the rest of us are not?" Lady Sula's eyes narrowed at me. "People who are hurt only hurt others. And those who would seek to make it better always come to a point where they are either hurt more themselves or they can't do anything for the person in trouble."

"We should learn to deal with our own pain, then," I said. "It's wrong to use Bloodmagic."

"If you want a perfect life, your pain has to go somewhere." She shook her head. "You don't know anything about suffering, or about human life, do you?"

"I know it's wrong to make people suffer who don't deserve it."

"We all deserve it, Skyla." Lady Sula's eyes darkened. "We are all incapable of perfection, and those cracks in the human heart are not able to be repaired without blood and sacrifice. The City's shards were designed to ensure the most happiness for the most people. Our system is still unfair, maybe, but at least there's no silly recognition or rules to follow like we had when we looked to religion or politics. We simply *are*. And we are all happy this way. It's pragmatic."

"You can't be pragmatic with people." I looked at Storm, as another tear fell from my eye. "She deserved better. She shouldn't have died."

"Neither should have the others who lost their lives tonight." Lady Sula handed Storm back to me. "Well, then, show me. What should we do, Skyla? What *can* we do?"

I looked around to see everyone was watching me.

Ai stood, shivering, surrounded by guards. Just a little way from him, Aidan's eyes were still downcast from Storm's death, and seeing him so disoriented, I wondered if he was thinking about death.

Death was the ultimate way to leave the City by the Sea.

I closed my eyes and saw Mother Annika, with her cheeks stained with tears, River's forehead as it dripped with blood, and Father Albert's eyes as they narrowed with hate.

I turned back to Ai, who looked up at the tower. In the moonlight, I saw his shard glisten with muted power, and I knew he wanted to go back and suffer for us.

It was at that realization that I squared my shoulders. My arms still cupped Storm tightly, but I walked up to Ai and stood before him.

"I know what to do," I said.

I gave Ai a kiss on the cheek. When I stepped back, I shifted Storm in my arms so I could pull out the shard from his forehead.

I had to work quickly, before the others could realize what I'd done, before it was too late to undo it. I quickly replaced my shard with his.

"Take me to the tower," I instructed Lady Sula. At the sight of the shard in my forehead, her mouth dropped open. Behind her, the other Elders exchanged thoughtful glances.

"What? No," Aidan yelled. He started to reach for me, but an Elder stepped up beside him and grabbed hold of him as Lady Sula nodded slowly.

"Do as she says," she agreed, and then I was pushed and prodded as I was taken to the tower room and placed in Ai's former cell. Through everything, I felt Storm's body bounce against me, as my new shard began to hum, burning into me with a fierceness that overwhelmed me. I looked all around, to see the red spirals of light appearing all around me. For a long moment, I was scared, but as I stood there, holding onto Storm, I was able to relax some.

I was doing the right thing.

"Skyla!"

Aidan shoved past the Elders and stood before me. "Don't do this, please," he said. "Stay with me."

"I will always be with you." I reached out, the same as he'd once reached out to me, the same as Ai had reached for me before. "There's no one I'll ever love as I love you."

"I will find a way to free you," Aidan vowed, and he grabbed hold of my arm, much like I'd done to Ai earlier.

I shook my head. "It doesn't matter," I promised, even as I began to feel the shard's connection to the Community's ills. A pain rose up in my forehead around my new shard. "I need you to take care of Ai for me. Please."

"Skyla, no," Aidan shouted. "This isn't right. You shouldn't suffer for me to be happy."

"It's okay." I pressed my fingers into his shard. I could hear the whirring sound it made, as the power of the Bloodmagic I felt all around me pressed into him, and I began to use that power to subdue him.

Already the Aidan I loved was disappearing, as the Bloodmagic took hold of me, and I sought to take on his all pain and troubles.

I saw all his memories of us together as I took them away from him—I took as many as I could, but despite everything, he still fought me.

I stepped back from him, but he did not move away from me.

"No," he said. His voice was more stoic, but I knew from his eyes that he was still determined to remain next to me, even as his heart was breaking.

The pain from others started to overwhelm me, and I saw the shadows. There was a rift between love and fear, life and death, pain and ecstasy; I had stepped inside of it, and my body and mind were being torn apart by the raging battle of the shadows.

But there was more. I had only seen the shadows before; now, on the other side, I was face to face with only light.

"Oh, Aidan." I gave him a small smile before I saw his gaze go slack. "I feel so much love."

C. S. Johnson is an award-winning, genre-hopping author of science fiction and fantasy adventures such as *The Starlight Chronicles, The Order of the Crystal Daggers, The Divine Space Pirates,* and more. With a gift for sarcasm and an apologetic heart, she currently lives in Atlanta with her family. Find out more at https://www.csjohnson.me.

READING SAMPLE

from

THE HEIGHTS OF PERDITION

BOOK ONE OF *THE DIVINE SPACE PIRATES*

♦♦♦♦

C. S. Johnson

♦1♦

At just the right angle, the dark blue and white orb, suspended in a sea of invisible shadows, held in place by a faith as impossible to believe in as it was to see, fit nicely between his fingers. Outside his window, Earth looked small and fragile, seemingly innocent, and mostly harmless. A hollowness slipped between his thumb and forefinger as he squashed them together, crushing the blueberry-sized circle.

Amused by the irony of the forced perspective before him, a rare, genuine smile formed on Exton Shepherd's face.

It was, he decided, almost a shame no one else was around to witness such an unusual event. He smooshed his fingers together, imagining the world completely decimated into dust.

But then, he recalled, he'd given plenty of smiles earlier, as all the hubbub went on about the ship. Surely the crew, his hodgepodge of adopted family and coworkers, would have been satisfied with those, even though they were inauthentic at best and mocking at worst.

Duty sometimes demanded playing happy. Exton knew that, and he followed it, even in instances he loathed.

Like today.

Between the thirteenth and fifteenth sunrises of his day, he'd watched the only other person he truly cared for in all the world—no, he mentally corrected himself, in all the universe—pledge her love, heart, and life to another man.

It was heartbreaking on some levels, but strangely freeing, too.

The wedding had been quaint, warm, and sweet. Its simplicity suggested nothing of its socially taxing nature.

Exton had no regrets about ducking out as soon as the bride and groom finished their vows and the Ecclesia had pronounced them husband and wife.

Once he had successfully slipped out of sight, Exton proceeded to the Captain's Lounge, the small room he'd claimed as his the day after launching the *Perdition* into space. There was little to be said of the room's comfort; it was more like a tall elevator shaft than a room, empty of everything but the coldness of space and a small window hidden up near the far end. More than once, Exton wondered if he'd found a kind of kinship with it; hollow and bleak, with a tiny view looking out toward the fleeing horizon.

It was there, on a window seat built into the windowpane, where Exton tucked his legs under his chin and entered into his own world of privacy, where he was free to be who he wanted, even if it was for only a moment.

As captain of the ship, he didn't want his crew to see him in one of his more melancholy moods.

His frown returned when he opened his fingers again, only to see Earth was still hanging in space before him, its silence mocking and spiteful. Rearranging his hand, he made it seem like he was carrying the earth in the palm. Fleetingly, he toyed with the idea of pretending to toss the small pearl away into the dark recesses of space, into an imaginary hell.

But he knew that would not work.

Exton knew two things with startling clarity and unshakable certainty: The first was that hell was real, and the second was that it was his home.

"Having fun?" a voice asked from below him.

"Huh?" Exton jerked around in surprise, nearly falling off the window ledge. "Come on, Emery, don't do that," he groaned, while the young woman dressed all in white only laughed. His balance, already compromised by the pull of the starship's gravity, faltered again as Exton tried to adjust himself. "You know I don't like it when people interrupt me, especially when I'm here."

"But it's my wedding day," Emery insisted. "And I'd like to have a dance with the ship's captain before the night shift starts. Come on, we're up first."

Exton gave up on staying by the window and jumped down as gracefully as he could. "All the shifts up here are technically the night shift," he grumbled.

"Some would say we live in perpetual day up here on the *Perdition*," Emery offered, her voice gentle even as she maintained her stance. "Sunrise and sunset are only ninety-two minutes apart for us now, when we're this close to Earth."

"Sunrises and sunsets do not make day and night up here," Exton told her, touching his forehead.

Emery reached out and took his hand, before she placed it over his heart. "I think your problem is too much night in here, not out there." She turned her attention back to the window, where six inches of steel-grade glass separated them from the vacuum of space.

Exton followed her gaze, wondering if she was looking for any sign of familiarity from their old home. He watched as the end of the ocean braced itself against the shore of the Old Republic; he felt his memory pull him in, and he could see it clearly inside his mind.

The chill of the old mountains where he would go work and play with his father, the spray of the salt water on his transport module, the warmth of his mother's arms as she welcomed him home from school—all of it embraced him, surrounding him and penetrating into the deep recesses of his heart.

And then there was pain, and then it was gone.

Exton shook his head. "I know it seems like a long time has passed, but it's time to cause the URS some trouble. It's almost the anniversary, you know."

"I know," she replied. A sudden sadness appeared in her gaze, and Exton wondered if she had been reminiscing as well.

Pushing aside his grief, he straightened his shoulders. "I have a plan that will really make them sorry this year, Em."

"I know you're a man of your word," Emery replied, "but I'm not sure it will be enough to convince them to give us what we want."

"They already cannot give us what we want." Exton shrugged. "Our game was never for power. It was for meaning."

"It's not a game, Exton."

"I know it's not!" Out of the corner of his eye, he saw Emery flinch. "I know it's not," he repeated carefully, reverting to his usual, detached tone. "It's not our fault that it became a quest for survival, Emery. I know that even more than you do."

"If it's survival you want," Emery scoffed, "there's no point in selling your soul in the process."

Before Exton could assure Emery he had no soul left that was worth saving, let alone selling, he stopped. Happy times, he reminded himself.

Emery's wedding was a special occasion, one that had excited her for the past several months, offering a glimmer of hope on a horizon of gloom and turmoil. Exton was determined not to let the past rob him—or her—of anything else, so long as it was in his power. "You're right," he acquiesced, momentarily giving in.

Emery smiled brightly, and Exton suddenly had a hard time believing she was only two years younger than he was. At twenty-two, she seemed much more innocent than the figure that gazed back at him when he looked in the mirror.

He slipped his hand out from under hers, before taking and squeezing it. "Are you sure you wouldn't like to have the first dance with your new husband?"

"Tyler is my heart's desire," Emery told him firmly, "but you will always be my hero."

Exton grimaced. He knew he was no hero. "It would be a shame to waste your time with me."

"Time with you is not a waste."

"Did Tyler approve of changing up the dancing order? The man might be in love, but there's no need to make him prove to be the fool."

"Hey, Tyler's your commander, and your best friend," Emery objected. "You know he's not a fool."

"Not where it concerns you. He would be smart to correct that, and I have been telling him since he received approval from the Ecclesia to start courting you," Exton told her. He gave her a devious look. "Should I make him walk the plank?"

Emery frowned and searched the darkened shadows of his face. "That's not funny, Exton."

"I know."

They walked in silence for a few moments before Exton spoke once more. "I don't want to dance. No offense, Em."

"Traditionally, it was the daughter's duty to dance with her father, first." Emery smiled. "But that's more of a cultural thing I've read about from the Old Republic."

"Yes, I remember that," Exton agreed. "Ironic, how the Revolutionary States would be appalled by it now."

Of course, he recalled, even the idea of using the term "father" might have some of the more militant protestors up in arms, as the beloved Daddy Dictator of the URS, Grant Osgood, did not encourage familial relationships, unless such feelings were directed toward government.

"If the URS is against it, you should be more inclined to appease me, then," Emery contended.

There was a breath of silence and stillness before Exton responded. "I'm not our father," he scoffed.

"You're more like him than you might wish."

As Exton scowled at her, Emery pointed her finger at him accusingly. "See? You even have the same exasperated look he used to get when he was frustrated."

"I'll have to take your word for it." Exton shrugged, scratching his head. He frowned as he realized it had been some time since he'd gotten a haircut. His father used to do the same thing, especially when he was planning his next engineering endeavor. Exton suddenly wondered if it was his own scruffy locks that had been making him shrink back from mirrors of late.

He missed his father too much to want to see him staring out of the mirror from the other side of the grave.

Emery chuckled again, drawing him out of his thoughts. "Well, I know at least one trait you share with him. He had a hard time telling me no to anything I wanted, if memory serves."

"You look too much like Mom for me to say no," Exton admitted. "I'm sure he had the same problem, but that's one I'm more willing to share with him."

With her dark brown hair, blue-green eyes, and petite form, Emery was the living memory of their mother. She even had the same dimple hovering above the left corner of her lips, a trait Exton knew was the extent of their common features. Their father's blue eyes, as clear and sharp as ice, had passed to him, along with his height, broad shoulders, and black hair.

"He always did want me to follow in his footsteps," Exton muttered as they headed out of the Captain's Lounge. "But I'm not sure he would have enjoyed the ghost of Captain Chainsword, the infamous space lumberjack pirate."

"I don't think he would have liked it, given how much he derided you for enjoying those fantasy adventures you used to read."

"It seemed fitting at the time, to create a new role for him to play, along with the rest of us."

"I suppose." Emery shrugged. "But Papa was a brilliant engineer, same as you, and a good man. I'm not sure he would have liked your emphasis on piracy and power."

"For the most part, I think you are right," Exton agreed. "But he was too idealistic by far. That was what got him killed." He looked out a nearby window, where, even as he could no longer see Earth, he still felt the pull of its shadow.

"In hindsight, you would prove to be correct on that point."

"That is why I will not make the same mistake as he did. While *Paradise* is out of reach, *Perdition* will do what it can to ensure a better life for us."

"And others, too," Emery added proudly.

"Maybe." Exton shrugged. "I only have a duty to you, and you're technically Tyler's problem now. Anyone else is just extra."

"Your duty to me hasn't ended."

Exton rolled his eyes. "I'm going to dance with you, aren't I? What else is there?"

"Your duty to me might include a dance tonight, but I wish for you to find someone you would love as I love Tyler." She smiled. "Someone you can spend your life trying to make happy."

"Even as life makes me miserable?"

Emery frowned and sighed. "I don't know why you do that."

"Do what?"

"Make it impossible for yourself to be happy."

"Happiness is fleeting, remember?" Exton rolled his eyes. "Even the leaders of the Ecclesia would agree with me there."

"They don't often agree with you, especially when it comes to your mandates," Emery concurred. "The only reason they would on this account is because the phrasing is vague enough to seem to agree on the meaning." She narrowed her gaze. "And the practice."

Exton wrinkled his nose. "We've been up here for too long if you know me so well."

"I still prefer this to when we were off at different universities, working on our studies," Emery admitted with a thoughtful smile. "But as for the argument, you don't seem to agree with the Ecclesia a whole lot, either. You don't share most of their beliefs. I find it hard to believe that you would try to garner support from among their teachings."

"Their teachings on wisdom and life, and how it should be, I respect. But it's different when you're trying to manage a pirate starship and ruin an empire."

"Not to mention when you insist so stubbornly on remaining miserable."

"I *am* going back to your wedding celebration, aren't I?" Exton groaned. "Please don't push it, Em. You know how I feel. If God would grant your wish for me, if he wanted so much for me to be 'happy,' he could have let me 'fall in love' with someone on the *Perdition*, like you and Tyler. But even when we send our smaller ships down to Earth for supplies, see Aunt Patty, or attack the URS, there's no one there for me. There are only people there who want the protection *Perdition* can offer to political dissents or refugees such as themselves."

After a moment of thought, he added, "Besides, my job is to protect and lead aboard the spaceship. The last thing I need is to be led around by the whims of a woman."

"There's no need to make it sound so deplorable," Emery scoffed, arching an eyebrow at him. "Do you honestly think dealing with the moods of a man are any easier?"

He flashed her a charming grin.

"You don't need to set yourself up for failure like that. We have only been up in space for six years now, hiding in the shadows of all the toxic clouds while playing war games with the URS."

"Not to mention watching destruction of all other sorts go unchecked," Exton added, his voice grim.

"It's not all 'unchecked,'" Emery reminded him. "Exton, you still can't lose hope. God is a supposed to be a god of miracles, remember? We have time."

Exton wondered how his sister could be worried about his heart, when his life, as well all the lives of his crew, faced the bigger risk. It was one thing to be aware of danger, but another to disregard it, especially for something as silly as true love.

He studied Emery's daydreaming smile in silence and decided he had the right of it: As much as she was ever his practical and precise sister, Emery's wedded bliss was affecting her judgment.

Exton was surprised at the sudden stab of jealousy. He squashed it down as he caught sight of the approaching Earth through the galley windows.

Didn't Emery see the coming battle? Exton wondered. *Didn't she feel the haunted air about the starship, with specters of the past lurking around every corner of the* Perdition?

They couldn't outlast the URS forever up in space. While Exton and the Ecclesia had established the *Perdition* as a safe haven over the past few years, it was only a matter of time before the URS would come for them, and he knew it would not be to make peace.

"What is it, Exton?" Emery asked, jolting him out of his gloomy thoughts.

Exton sighed. "It's not like God's just going to dump someone into the ship just for me. You might as well save your breath for dancing, Em."

Thank you for reading! Please leave a review for this book and check out my other books for more adventures!

CPSIA information can be obtained
at www.ICGtesting.com
Printed in the USA
LVHW090218170521
687116LV00001BA/39